Our House on the Hill

Philippe Dupasquier

PUFFIN BOOKS

January

February

March

April

May

June

July

August

September

October

November

December

Some Other Picture Puffins

DEAR DADDY . . . *Philippe Dupasquier*
THE SANDAL *Tony Bradman / Philippe Dupasquier*
GOING WEST *Martin Waddell / Philippe Dupasquier*
THE SNOW QUEEN *Hans Andersen / Errol Le Cain*
GUMDROP FINDS A GHOST *Val Biro*
BORKA *John Burningham*
THE ENORMOUS CROCODILE *Roald Dahl / Quentin Blake*
MOOSE *Michael Foreman*
ANGELINA BALLERINA *Katharine Holabird / Helen Craig*
HIAWATHA'S CHILDHOOD *Henry Wadsworth Longfellow / Errol Le Cain*
MOTHER GOOSE COMES TO CABLE STREET *Rosemary Stones / Andrew Mann*
THE SUPERMARKET MICE *Margaret Gordon*
THE LITTLE TRAIN *Graham Greene / Edward Ardizzone*
DON'T FORGET THE BACON! *Pat Hutchins*
RHYMES AROUND THE DAY *Jan Ormerod*
ON FRIDAY SOMETHING FUNNY HAPPENED *John Prater*
I'M COMING TO GET YOU! *Tony Ross*
TEDDY BEAR POSTMAN *Phoebe and Selby Worthington*